Read on for an extract of another
brilliant Harriet Evans novel,

Love
Always

PROLOGUE

Cornwall, 1963

If you close your eyes, perhaps you can still see them. As they were that sundrenched afternoon, the day everything changed.

Outside the house, in the shadows by the terrace, when they thought no one was looking. Mary is in the kitchen making chicken salad and singing along to Music While You Work *on the Home Service. There's no one else around. It's the quiet before lunch, too hot to do anything.*

'Come on,' she says. She is laughing. 'Just one cigarette, and then you can go back up.' She chatters her little white teeth together, her pink lips wet. 'I won't bite, promise.'

He looks anxiously around him. 'All right.'

She has her back to him as she picks her way confidently through the black brambles and grey-green reeds, down the old path that leads to the sea. Her glossy hair is caught under the old green-and-yellow towel she has wrapped round her neck. He follows, nervously.

He's terrified of these encounters – terrified because he knows they're wrong, but still he wants them, more than he's wanted anything in his life. He wants to feel her honey-soft skin, to let his hand move up her thigh, to nuzzle her neck, to hear her cool, cruel laugh. He has known a couple of women: eager, rough-haired girls

1

at college, all inky fingers and beery breath, but this is different. He is a boy compared to her.

Oh, he knows it's wrong, what they're doing. He knows his head has been turned, by the heat, the long, light evenings, the intoxicating, almost frightening, sense of liberation here at Summercove, but he just doesn't care. He feels truly free at last.

The world is becoming a different place, there's something happening this summer. A change is coming, they can all feel it. And that feeling is especially concentrated here, in the sweet, lavender-soaked air of Summercove, where the crickets sing long into the night and where the Kapoors let their guests, it would seem, do what on earth they want . . . Being there is like being on the inside of one of those glass domes you have as a child, visible to the outside world, filled with glitter, waiting to be shaken up. The Kapoors know it too. They are all moths, drawn to the flickering candlelight.

'Hurry up, darling,' she says, almost at the bottom of the steps now, in the bright light, the white dots on her blue polka-dot swimming costume dancing before his eyes. He clings to the rope handle, terrified once more. The steps are dark and slippery, cut into the cliffs and slimy with algae. She watches him, laughing. She often makes him feel ridiculous. He's never been around bohemian people before. All his life, even now, he has been used to having rules, being told when to wash behind his ears, when to hand an essay in, used to the smell of sweaty boys – now young men – queuing for meals, changing for cricket. He's at the top of the pile, knows his place there, he's secure in that world.

He justifies it by saying this is different. It's one last hurrah, and he means to make the most of it, even if it is terrifying . . . He stumbles on a slippery step as she watches him from the beach, a cigarette dangling from her lip. His knee gives way beneath him, and for one terrifying moment he thinks he will fall, until he slams his other leg down, righting himself at the last minute.

'Careful, darling,' she drawls. 'Someone's going to get killed on those steps if they're not careful.'

Shaken, he reaches the bottom, and she comes towards him, handing him a cigarette, laughing. 'So clumsy,' she says, and he hates her in that moment, hates how sophisticated and smooth she is, so heedless of what she's doing, how wrong it is . . . He takes the cigarette but does not light it. He pulls her towards him instead, kissing her wet, plump pink lips, and she gives a little moan, wriggling her slim body against his. He can feel himself getting hard already, and her fingers move down his body, and he pushes her against the rock, and they kiss again.

'Have you always been this bad?' he asks her afterwards, as they are smoking their cigarettes. The heat of the sun is drying the sweat on their bodies. They lie together on the tiny beach, sated, as the waves crash next to them. A lost sandal, relic of someone else's wholly innocent summer day, is bobbing around at the edge of the tide. The cigarette is thick and rancid in his mouth. Now it's over, as ever, he is feeling sick.

She turns to him. 'I'm not bad.'

He thinks she is. He thinks she is evil, in fact, but he can't stay away from her. She smiles slowly, and he says, without knowing why he needs to say it, 'Look, it's been lots of fun. But I think it's best if—' He trails off. 'Break it off.'

Her face darkens for a second. 'You pompous ass.' She laughs, sharply. '"Break it off"? Break what off? There's nothing to break off. This isn't . . . anything.'

He is aware that he sounds stupid. 'I thought we should at least discuss it. Didn't want to give you the—' God, he wishes it were over. He finds himself giving her a little nod. 'Give you the wrong impression.'

'Oh, that's very kind of you.' She stubs the cigarette into the wet sand, and stands up, pulling the towel off the ground and around her again. He can't tell if she's angry or relieved, or – what? This is all beyond him, and it strikes him again that he's glad it will be over and that soon he can go back to being himself again, boring, ordinary, out of all this, normal.

'It's been—' he begins.

'Oh, fuck you,' she says. 'Don't you dare.' She turns to go, but as she does something comes tumbling down the steps. It is a small piece of black slate.

And then there is a noise, a kind of thudding. Footsteps.

'Who's there?' he says, looking up, but after the white light of the midday sun it is impossible to see anyone on the dark steps.

In the long years afterwards, when he never spoke about this summer, what happened, he would ask himself – because there was no one else he could ask: Who? His wife? His family? Hah – if he'd been wrong about what he'd seen. For, in that moment, he'd swear he could make out a small foot, disappearing back up onto the path to the house.

He turns back to her. 'Damn. Was that someone, do you think?'

She sighs. 'No, of course not. The path's crumbling, that's all. You're paranoid, darling.' She says lightly, 'As if they'd ever believe it of you, anyway. Calm down. Remember, we're supposed to be grown-ups. Act like one.'

She puts one hand on the rope and hauls herself gracefully up. 'Bye, darling,' she says, and he watches her go. 'Don't worry,' she calls. 'No one's going to find out. It's our little secret.'

But someone did. Someone saw it all.

PART ONE

February 2009

CHAPTER ONE

It is 7:16 a.m.

The train to Penzance leaves at seven-thirty. I have fourteen minutes to get to Paddington. I stand in a motionless Hammersmith and City line carriage, clutching the overhead rail so hard my fingers ache. I have to catch this train; it's a matter of life and death.

Quite literally, in fact – my grandmother's funeral is at two-thirty today. You're allowed to be an hour late for dinner, but you can't be an hour late for a funeral. It's a once-in-a-lifetime deal.

I've lived in London all my life. I know the best places to eat, the bars that are open after twelve, the coolest galleries, the prettiest spots in the parks. And I know the Hammersmith and City line is useless. I hate it. Why didn't I leave earlier? Impotent fury washes through me. And still the carriage doesn't move.

This morning, the sound of pattering rain on the quiet street woke me while it was still dark. I haven't been sleeping for a while, since before Granny died. I used to complain bitterly about my husband Oli's snoring, how he took up the whole bed, lying prone in a diagonal line. He's been away for nearly two weeks now. At first I thought it'd be good, if only because I could catch up on sleep, but I haven't. I lie awake, thoughts racing through my head, one wide-awake side of my brain taunting the other, which is begging for rest. I feel mad. Perhaps I am mad. Although they say if you think you're going mad that definitely means you're not. I'm not so sure.

7:18 a.m. I breathe deeply, trying to calm down. It'll be OK. It'll all be OK.

Granny died in her sleep last Friday. She was eighty-nine. The funny thing is, it still shocked me. Booking my train tickets to come down to Cornwall, in February, it seemed all wrong, as though I was in a bad dream. I spoke to Sanjay, my cousin, over the weekend and he said the same thing. He also said, 'Don't you want to punch the next person in the face who says, "Eighty-nine? Well, she had a good innings, didn't she?" Like she deserved to die.'

I laughed, even though I was crying, and then Jay said, 'I feel like something's coming to an end, don't you? Something bigger than all of us.'

It made me shiver, because he is right. Granny was the centre of everything. The centre of my life, of our family. And now she's gone, and – I can't really explain it. She was the link to so many things. She was Summercove.

We're at Edgware Road, and it's 7:22 a.m. I might get it. I just might still get the train.

Granny and Arvind, my grandfather, had planned for this moment. Talked about it quite openly, as if they wanted everyone to be clear about what they wanted, perhaps because they didn't trust my mother or my uncle – Jay's dad – to follow their wishes. I'd like to believe that's not true, but I'm afraid it probably is. They specified what would happen when either one of them died first, what happens to the paintings in the house, the trust that is to be set up in Granny's memory, the scholarship that is funded in Arvind's memory, and what happens to Summercove.

Arvind is ninety. He is moving into a home. Louisa, my

mother's cousin, has taken charge of that. Louisa has taken charge of the funeral, too. She likes taking charge. She has picked everything that Granny didn't leave instructions about, from the hymns to the fillings in the sandwiches for the wake afterwards (a choice of egg mayonnaise, curried chicken or cucumber). Her husband, the handsome but extremely boring Bowler Hat, will be handing out the orders of service at the funeral and topping up drinks at the wake. Louisa is organising everything, and it is very kind of her, but we feel a bit left out, Jay and I. As ever, the Leighton side of the family has got it right, with their charming English polo-shirts-and-crumpets approach to life and we, the Kapoors, are left looking eccentric, disjointed, odd. Which I suppose we are.

Cousin Louisa is also in charge of packing up the house. For Summercove is to be sold. Our beautiful white art deco house perched between the fields and the sea in Cornwall will soon be someone else's. It is where Granny and my grandfather lived for fifty years, raised their children. I spent every summer of my life there. It's really the only home I've ever known and I'm the only one, it seems, who's sentimental about it, who can't bear to see it go. Mum, my uncle Archie, Cousin Louisa – even my grandfather – they're all brisk about it. I don't understand how they can be.

'Too many memories here,' Granny used to say when she'd talk about it, tell us firmly what was going to happen. 'Time for someone else to make some.'

Finally. The doors wobble open at Paddington and I rush out and run up the steps, pushing past people, muttering, 'Sorry, sorry.' Thank God it's the Hammersmith and City line – the exit opens right onto the vast concourse of the station. It is 7:28. The train leaves in two minutes.

The cold air hits me. I jab my ticket frantically in the barrier and run down the stairs to the wide platform, legs like jelly as I tumble down, faster and faster. I am nearly there, nearly at the bottom . . . I glance up at the big clock. 7:29. Like a child, I jump the last three steps, my knees nearly giving way underneath me, and leap onto the train. I stand by the luggage racks, panting, trying to collect myself. There is a final whistle, the sound of doors slamming further along the endless snake of carriages. We are off.

I find a seat and sit down. My mother doesn't drive, so I know the ways of the train. The key to a good journey is not a table seat. I never understand why you would get one unless you knew everyone round the table. You end up spending five hours playing awkward footsie with a sweaty middle-aged man, or surrounded by a screaming, overexcited family. I slot myself into a window seat and close my eyes. A cool trickle of sweat slides down my backbone.

This is the train I took every summer, with Mum, to Summercove. Mum would bring me down, stay for a few days and then leave before the rest of her relatives arrived, and sometimes – but not often – before she and Granny could row about something: money, men, me.

It was always so much fun, the train down to Penzance when I was little. It was the anticipation of the holiday ahead, six weeks in Cornwall, six weeks with my favourite people in my favourite place. Mum would be in a strangely good mood on the train down, and so would I, both of us looking forward to diluting our twosome for a few weeks, away from our dark Hammersmith mansion flat, where the wallpaper peeled away from the walls, and in the summer the smell from the bins outside was noticeable. Bryant Court didn't suit summer. The noises inside and out got worse, scratching and strange, and the cast of characters in the building seemed to get less eccentric and more menacing. The hot weather seemed to dry them out, to make them more brittle and screeching. We were always euphoric to be out of there, away from it all.

Once, when we were on our way to Paddington and my mother was dragging me by the wrist towards a waiting cab, bags slung over our shoulders, Mrs Pogorzelski hissed, 'Slut!' at Mum, as she opened the door. I didn't know what it meant, or why she was saying it. Mum bundled me into the black cab and we sat there grinning, surrounded by luggage, as we rolled up through Kensington towards the station, both of us complicit in some way that I couldn't define. That was also one of the times Mum forgot her purse, and the cab driver let us have a ride for free after she cried. She forgot her purse quite often, my mother.

She is at Summercove already, helping Cousin Louisa sort out the funeral and the house. She is convinced Louisa has her eye on some pieces of furniture already, convinced she is controlling everything. Archie, Mum's twin brother and Jay's dad, is there too. Mum and her cousin do not get on. But then Mum and a lot of people don't get on.

The train is flying through the outskirts of London, out past Southall and Heathrow, through scrubby wasteland that doesn't know whether it's town or countryside, towards Reading. I look around me for the first time since collapsing into my seat. I want a coffee, and I should have something to eat, though I'm not quite sure I can eat anything.

'Tickets, please,' says a voice above me. I jump, more violently than is warranted and the ticket inspector looks at me in alarm. I hand him my tickets – thankfully, I collected them at Liverpool Street, knowing the queues at Paddington would be horrendous. I blink, trying not to shake, as the desire to be sick, to faint, anything, sweeps over me again, and slump back against the scratchy seat, watching the inspector. He raises his eyebrows as he checks them over.

'Long way to be going for the day.'

'Yes,' I say. He looks at me, and I find myself saying, too eagerly, 'I have to be back in London tomorrow. There's an appointment first thing – I have an appointment I can't miss.'

He nods, but already I've given him too much information,

and I can feel myself flushing with shame. He's a Londoner, he doesn't want to chat. The trouble is, I want to talk to someone. I need to. A stranger, someone who I won't see again.

I haven't told my family I'm coming back tonight. Growing up with my mother, I learned long ago that the less you say, the less you get asked. The one person I would like to confide in is being buried today, in the churchyard at St Mary's, a tiny stone hut, so old people aren't sure when it was first built. In the churchyard there is the grave of a customs officer, one of many killed by desperate smugglers. There is a lot about Cornwall that is still kind of wild, pagan, and though the fish restaurants, tea shops and surfboards cover some of it up, they can't entirely conceal it.

Granny believed that. She was from Cornwall, she grew up near St Ives, on the wild north coast. She saw Alfred Wallis painting by the docks, she was born with the cry of seagulls and the wind whistling through the winding streets of the old town in her ears. She loved the landscape of her home county; it was her life, her job. She lived most of her life there, did her best work there, sitting in her studio high at the top of the house, overlooking the sea.

There are so many things I never asked her, and now I wish I had. So often that I wished I could confide in her, about all sorts of things, but knew I couldn't. For much as I loved my granny, I was scared of her too, of the blank look she'd get in her lovely green eyes sometimes when she looked at me. My husband Oli said once he sometimes thought she could see straight into your soul, like a witch. He was joking, but he was a little scared of her, and I know what he meant. There are some things you didn't ask her. Some things she wouldn't ever talk about.

Because for many years, Summercove was a very different place, centre of a glittering social whirl, and my grandparents were wealthy, successful, and it seemed as if they had the world at their feet. But then their daughter Cecily died, two months short of her sixteenth birthday, and my grandmother stopped painting. She shut up her studio at the top of the house and, as far as I know, she never went back. I learned from a very early age never to ask why. Never to mention Cecily's name, even. There are no photos of her in the house, and no one ever talks about her. I know she died in 1963, and I know it was an accident of some kind, and I know Granny stopped painting after that, and that's about it.

We're going past Newbury, and the landscape is greener. There has been a lot of rain lately, and the rivers are swollen and brown under a grey sky. The fields are newly ploughed. A fast wind whips dead leaves over and around the train. I sit back and breathe out, feeling the nauseous knot of tension in my stomach start to slowly unravel, as a wave of something like calm washes over me. We are leaving London. We are getting closer.

Happily Ever After

You can't escape the ties that bind. The past catches up with you no matter how far you try to run...

This is a story of a girl who doesn't believe in happy endings. Or happy families. It's the story of Eleanor Bee, a shy, book-loving girl who vows to turn herself into someone bright, shiny and confident, someone sophisticated. Someone who knows how life works.

Harriet Evans

'Funny, wistful and wise...I loved this book'
Katie Fforde

Happily Ever After

IN REAL LIFE,
NOTHING IS EVER THAT SIMPLE...

But life has a funny way of catching us unawares.
Turns out that Elle doesn't know everything about love.
Or life. Or how to keep the ones we love safe...

Absorbing, poignant and unforgettable,
Happily Ever After is a compelling
story of a fractured family and a girl
who doesn't believe in love.